PRINCESS NAOMI HELPS A UNICORN

ONCE UPON A Dance

ILLUSTRATED BY ETHAN ROFFLER

Dedicated to kids whose best friend is their sister or brother (at least most of the time).

Princess Naomi Helps a Unicorn
A Dance-It-Out Creative Movement Story for Young Movers

© 2021 *Once Upon a Dance*

Illustrated by Ethan Roffler, www.storiesuntoldservices.com

All 2021 sales donated to ballet companies struggling under COVID-19.

This charming volume from the Dance-It-Out series introduces readers to Princess Naomi.
Fed up with her annoying sister, Naomi storms out of the castle, only to discover a unicorn in need of help.
With a sense of purpose and compassion, she quickly forgets her anger.
Ballerina Konora helps readers connect with movement and explore dance fundamentals.

ISBN: 978-1-7365-8992-2 (paperback); 978-1-7368-7505-6 (ebook); 978-1-7368-7506-3 (hardcover)
Juvenile Fiction: Imagination & Play (Performing Arts: Dance) (Animals: Dragons, Unicorns & Mythical)
First Edition

Other **Once Upon a Dance** Titles:

Joey Finds His Jump!: A Dance-It-Out Creative Movement Story for Young Movers
Petunia Perks Up: A Dance-It-Out Movement and Meditation Story
Danny, Denny, and the Dancing Dragon: A Dance-It-Out Creative Movement Story for Young Movers
Princess Naomi Helps a Unicorn: A Dance-It-Out Creative Movement Story for Young Movers
The Cat with the Crooked Tail: A Dance-It-Out Creative Movement Story for Young Movers
Brielle's Birthday Ball: A Dance-It-Out Creative Movement Story for Young Movers
Mira Monkey's Magic Mirror Adventure: A Dance-It-Out Creative Movement Story for Young Movers
Belluna's Big Adventure in the Sky: A Dance-It-Out Creative Movement Story for Young Movers
Danika's Dancing Day: A Dance-It-Out Creative Movement Story for Young Movers
Sadoni Squirrel: Superhero: A Dance-It-Out Creative Movement Story for Young Movers
Dancing Shapes: Ballet and Body Awareness for Young Dancers
More Dancing Shapes: Ballet and Body Awareness for Young Dancers
Nutcracker Dancing Shapes: Shapes and Stories from Konora's Twenty-Five Nutcracker Roles
Dancing Shapes with Attitude: Ballet and Body Awareness for Young Dancers
Konora's Shapes: Poses from Dancing Shapes for Creative Movement & Ballet Teachers
More Konora's Shapes: Poses from More Dancing Shapes for Creative Movement & Ballet Teachers
Ballerina Dreams Ballet Inspiration Journal/Notebook & Dancing Shapes Ballet Inspiration Journal/Notebook

Hello Fellow Dancer,

My name is Ballerina Konora.

I love stories, adventures, and ballet, and I'm glad you're here today!

Will you be my dancing partner and act out the story along with me and Naomi?

I've included descriptions of movements that express the story. You can decide whether to use these ideas or create your own moves. Be safe, of course, and do what works for you in your space. And if you want to settle in and enjoy the pictures first, that's fine.

Konora

P.S. You don't have to be a princess to act like Naomi. And, boy or girl, you can dance like all of the characters and creatures in this story.

Once upon a dance, Princess Naomi lived in a castle along with the King, the Queen, and her sister, Princess Miranda. Naomi loved her home, and she appreciated all the extra space, especially during sister squabbles. Most of the time, the sisters' friendship was as solid as the castle rocks—made from the strongest stones in the kingdom. But this morning, the sisters had argued over every little thing.

Naomi celebrates the open feeling of the castle. Let's re-create this: I reach my chest to the sky and spin with my arms out wide. I feel my happiness expand into the wide world when I'm happy. Will you try this move with me? How does it make you feel?

I feel the opposite when I scrunch my body into the shape of those strong rocks. Can you squeeze yourself into a round rock shape? Imagine that if someone picked you up, you'd keep your shape. I feel powerful and strong when I activate my muscles.

It started at breakfast when Miranda spilled the milk, and there wasn't any left for Naomi's cereal. Then Miranda insisted on loudly singing Naomi's least favorite song. It was one thing after another, and Naomi felt like she might explode if she didn't walk away. She stormed out of the castle, closing the front door behind her with a satisfying thud.

Let's try to gather some pretend anger into our fists, our squeezed hands. Now, keep your tight fists as you walk like a thunderstorm with legs. Stomp your feet as you land, moving quickly with extra force.

And then, the pretend, in-the-air door slam!

Naomi headed straight to the stable to visit her horse named En Tournant. She knew seeing him would make her feel calm, and make her anger seem less important.

En Tournant was sweet, strong, and quirky. He could gallop forward, of course. But he sometimes galloped sideways, and even enjoyed spinning around, which is why he was named *En Tournant*, which means 'while turning' in French.

Let's pretend to gallop like En Tournant. *Chassé* is the French ballet term for galloping, and it means *to chase.* In this movement, one foot chases the other. Put one foot out in front and drag your other foot to meet it. Try it a little faster, bend your knees at the start, and straighten them as they come together.

We can also *chassé* sideways.

Finally, spin any way you like. *En Tournant* describes many different spinning moves.

En Tournant was fast. Crazy fast. Sometimes the princess imagined he had powerful wings slicing the air, as if flying was the only possible explanation for his speed. Galloping with the air whipping around her helped quiet her anger.

They were galloping along when she saw a purple dot in the distance. She guided En Tournant to check it out.

Can you flap your imaginary wings and practice those *chassés* again? Let's see if we can make bigger jumps this time. Keep using your knee bends to go down, then go up as if you're getting sucked up by a straw.

The purple dot turned out to be a unicorn! It was limp and droopy. The princess picked up one the unicorn's front legs. It just fell to the ground. She tried one of its hind legs, and the same thing happened. Naomi noticed poppy plants nearby. Hadn't the royal gardener said that poppies could make unicorns sleepy?

Naomi wasn't quite sure how to wake up the unicorn, but she hoped that some cold water might do the trick. She went to a nearby lake, scooped up some water, and took it back to the unicorn. Naomi slowly dripped it over the motionless body. Would the unicorn wake up? What would she do if it didn't move?

Let's be the unicorn and relax on the floor. Remember how we turned **on** all our muscles before? Now we're turning them **off.** It's difficult to do. You can ask someone to check whether your muscles are relaxed. Your limbs, meaning your arms and legs, should feel heavy when someone else lifts them.

Stand up, and let's be the princess getting the water. And relax again as the unicorn gets dripped on.

The unicorn instantly fluttered to life. It stood up, walked to the lake, and dipped its horn in, When it stood, its horn shone majestically.

The unicorn started drawing half circles in the dirt with its leg. Was it writing words? *What message did the unicorn have?* Naomi wondered.

Let's imagine we are the unicorn, and head over to the lake to dip our horns. Now feel the magical power as we reach our unicorn horns up to the ceiling.

Next, let's draw half circles in the sand with our toes. Start by reaching your foot in front of your body and move it around to the back, like you're writing a big C. See if you can point your toes, keep your legs straight, and reach your toes as far as you can without moving your hips.

The princess thought perhaps the unicorn was drawing a map, but she couldn't understand its meaning or destination. The princess told the unicorn, "I'll climb on your back, and you can take me where you want to go."

The unicorn came over, put its knees down on the ground, and held still. Naomi stretched her leg out to the side and climbed on.

And off they went!

First, we're the unicorn making a low shape.

Then character switch-a-roo:
We're the princess reaching our
leg up and over the unicorn.

The three of them went lightning-fast, leaping over bushes and puddles as they went. The path they traveled was just like the map that the unicorn had been trying to draw in the sand! Finally, the unicorn stopped near the entrance to a small cave.

It looked dark and creepy.

Woo hoo! Another chance for *chassés*. I love to quickly glide along. Giddy-up!

To leap over the bushes and puddles, reach your leg out like a kick then step-jump up and over the imaginary obstacles.

The unicorn whinnied. Naomi heard a response from inside, it sounded similar to the unicorn's call but at a higher pitch. Maybe it was a smaller unicorn? Was it trapped? The unicorn motioned for the princess to go inside. Naomi summoned her courage and headed in.

The cave had a low ceiling, so the princess hunched over. She felt like an elephant. Ouch! Naomi hit her head on something!

Let's reach our horn like the unicorn pointing the way.

Then down low we go, and waddle and sway like an elephant as we lean forward and head into the cave.

It was the ceiling, and it was getting lower the farther in she went. Naomi had to get on her hands and knees to continue. When the ceiling got even lower, she dropped down onto her belly and wiggled forward.

She could see a little light just ahead.

Put your hands and knees on the floor and crawl along like a baby. Now imagine you've bumped your head—how do you react?

Now lower yourself down even more. I feel like a seal, dragging my body along by pushing one elbow forward at a time.

The room opened up into a large cavern. Sunlight was streaming in through a small hole at the top. The good news was the ceiling was higher and Naomi was in an open space. The bad news was there was an upright cobra snake blocking her path, and it looked unhappy about being disturbed. The snake slowly turned its head, first one way, then the other. The princess took a breath for bravery, leapt over the cobra, and ran on.

At the height of her leap, she could see something purple across the room, just under where the light was coming in.

Let's be the snake. Lie on your belly and lift your head and back up, while trying to keep your hips on the ground. Gently turn your head to one side then the other.

Now back to being the Princess: leap over that snake and skedaddle away!

As Naomi got closer, she gasped. There, huddled in the corner was a baby unicorn. The princess scooped it up and quickly backtracked out of the cave.

We have to go back out of the cave in reverse order. Do you remember what to do? Over the snake, scoot like a seal, crawl like a baby, and sway like an elephant.

Phew, we made it!

Naomi brought the unicorn to its mother. The unicorn touched the baby with its horn, and a streak of light flowed out of the horn and into the little unicorn. The baby wiggled with delight.

With a nuzzle and a bow, the pair of unicorns thanked Naomi, then galloped away. Seeing the unicorns reunited warmed Naomi's heart, and it reminded her how grateful she was for her own family—even her sister. In fact, as she journeyed home on En Tournant, Naomi was surprised to realize that her anger at Miranda had disappeared.

Naomi was filled with happiness, and she couldn't wait to tell her sister about her incredible adventure!

Let's deliver the unicorn, wiggle with delight like the little one, and wave goodbye.

Thee end!
The end.

(My grandpa always ended stories this way, and I like to share his fun.)

Thanks for being my dance partner.
Until our next adventure.

Love,

Konora

Grown-ups can share that happy, helpful feeling by giving us a kind, honest review on Amazon or Goodreads 😉. We would be immensely grateful!

We are a COVID-sidelined mother and daughter pair who were both happily immersed in the ballet world until March, 2020. We hope by the time you read this, life is on its way back to normal. We wish you well.

THE DANCE-IT-OUT! COLLECTION

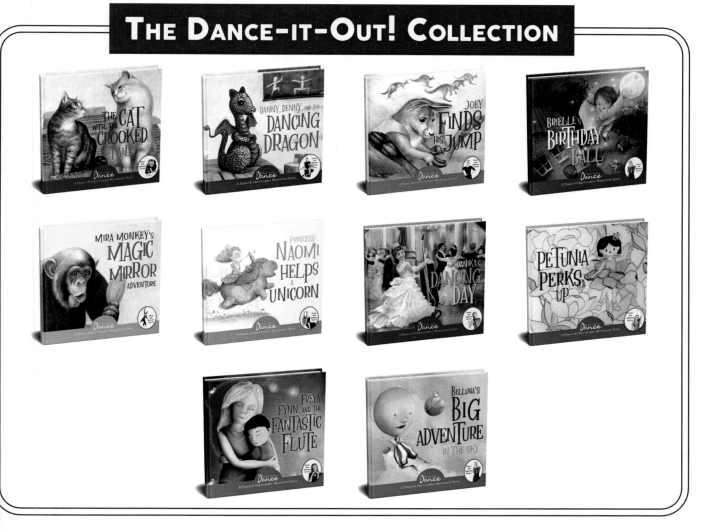

Made in United States
North Haven, CT
03 January 2022